3x+1

DR. DRABBLE'S
ASTOUNDING MUSICAL
MESMERIZER

Written by
Sigmund Brouwer and Wayne Davidson
Illustrated by
Bill Bell

VICTOR BOOKS®
A DIVISION OF SCRIPTURE PRESS PUBLICATIONS INC.
USA CANADA ENGLAND

With love, to
Donna

ISBN: 0-89693-904-9

© 1991 SP Publications, Inc. All
rights reserved.

VICTOR BOOKS
A division of SP Publications, Inc.
Wheaton, Illinois 60187

PJ and Chelsea were in Egypt on Dr. Drabble's Brilliant All-in-One Traveling Apparatus, a machine that was part ship, part bus, and part space shuttle.

There was always a surprise for PJ and Chelsea in Dr. Drabble's laboratory. He was a genius inventor and had an assistant named Arnie Clodbuckle.

This time, the surprise was a big, black snake. "Aaack!" PJ nearly jumped into the arms of his sister Chelsea.

The snake wrapped itself around PJ's leg.

Dr. Drabble smiled. "Now I will rescue you, PJ, with my Astounding Musical Mesmerizer." He grabbed a long tube that looked like a mixture between a trumpet and a flute.

He blew hard. Nothing happened.

"Oh, dear," Dr. Drabble said. "I seem to have miscalculated."

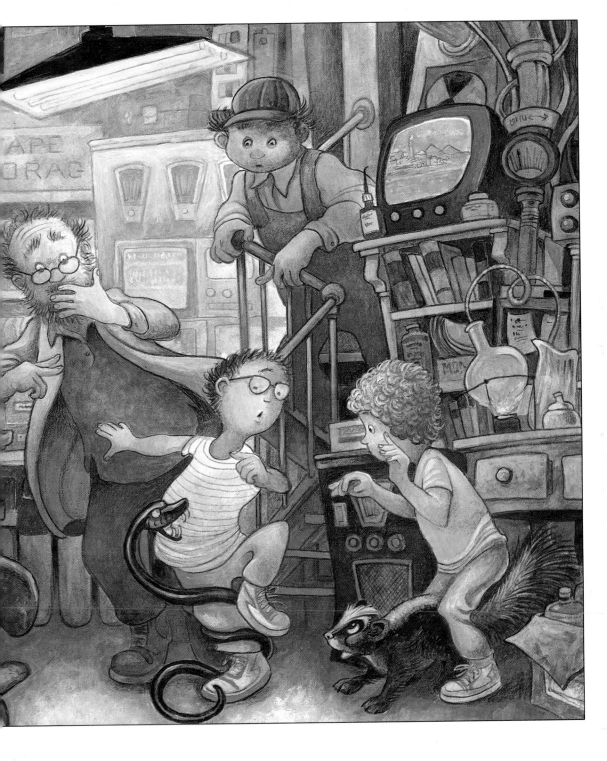

"I'm sorry," Doctor Drabble said. "I thought my Astounding Musical Mesmerizer would put the snake in a trance. Then I could order it to do anything."

He set the Astounding Musical Mesmerizer on his bench. Arnie took the snake off PJ's leg.

"Come on, Arnie," Dr. Drabble continued. "Let's go into town and find some parts to fix it." And they left.

PJ lifted the Astounding Musical Mesmerizer. A piece of cookie dropped from it onto the floor.

Chelsea took a close look. "Arnie's always eating in the laboratory." She stopped. "Hey! Maybe it was blocking the Astounding Musical Mesmerizer."

PJ blew on it. A long, soft melody came out the other end.

"Did you hear that?" he asked.

Chelsea replied very strangely. She said, "I will do whatever you command."

"Don't be silly. You never do anything I ask," PJ said.

"I will do whatever you command," Chelsea repeated.

"Then clean my room," PJ joked.

Chelsea started leaving.

"Hey!" PJ shouted. "It was only a joke. What's wrong with you?" Then he realized that she *was* mesmerized.

"I command you to be unmesmerized," PJ said. It was the only thing he could think of doing.

Chelsea began talking normally again. "What happened?" she asked.

PJ explained.

Then he had an idea. "I know how I can get revenge on Dr. Drabble and Arnie for scaring me with the snake."

PJ carried the Astounding Musical Mesmerizer, and left the laboratory with Chelsea and Wesley.

"Dr. Drabble and Arnie are going to the street markets of Cairo." PJ explained. "We'll find them there."

A little while later, PJ and Chelsea were able to sneak up on Dr. Drabble and Arnie.

PJ pulled out the Astounding Musical Mesmerizer and played it. Almost right away Dr. Drabble and Arnie turned around. They had strange looks on their faces.

"You are under my command," PJ whispered to them.

Dr. Drabble and Arnie nodded their heads.

"Good," PJ said gleefully. "This will teach you not to scare me again. First, jump up and down and stick your tongues out at each other."

Arnie and Dr. Drabble started jumping up and down. They stuck their tongues out at each other.

"Second," PJ said merrily, "walk down the street on your hands."

Dr. Drabble fell twice and Arnie fell five times, but finally they managed to walk down the street on their hands.

PJ and Chelsea ran along behind them, laughing all the way.

"Think of something," PJ told Chelsea. "It's your turn."

"Okay," she said. "I want you to sing 'Rock-a-Bye Baby.' Arnie must be the baby."

Arnie hopped into Dr. Drabble's arms. Dr. Drabble rocked him back and forth as he sang the whole lullaby.

PJ laughed and laughed. "This is the best revenge I've ever had!"

"Now," Chelsea giggled, "play Horsie. Arnie is the horse."

Arnie got on his hands and knees and neighed like a horse. Dr. Drabble climbed on his back.

"I've got a better idea," PJ said. "Let's ask them to give us a tour of Cairo!" He blew into the Astounding Musical Mesmerizer again to keep them under the spell.

"How often do you have to do that?" Chelsea asked.

"I don't know. Whenever I remember, I guess."

Chelsea took the Mesmerizer. "I'll blow it too," she said.

PJ turned to Dr. Drabble and Arnie. "Show us the city," he said sternly. "That will teach you for scaring me with a snake."

So off they went.

Dr. Drabble showed them the camels that were used to carry loads across the desert.

Dr. Drabble showed them old, old buildings where kings and queens used to live.

Dr. Drabble also showed them where many people still lived in tents made of animal hides.

And Dr. Drabble showed them the crowded marketplace where hundreds of shopkeepers shouted loudly as they tried to sell many things.

"Look at all these wonderful gifts," Chelsea said. "Can you mesmerize Dr. Drabble and Arnie into waiting here while we go spend our allowance?"

"Sure," said PJ. He commanded the two grown-ups to wait exactly where they were. "And don't say a word until we get back."

Unfortunately, while PJ and Chelsea were away shopping in the market-place, a fat and loud shopkeeper noticed that Dr. Drabble and Arnie were very quiet and still.

"Hey!" the shopkeeper shouted. "I have a deal for you."

Dr. Drabble and Arnie did not reply.

"Hey!" the shopkeeper shouted again. "Are you guys deaf?"

The shopkeeper went over and waved his hand in front of their faces. Dr. Drabble and Arnie did not blink.

"Mmm," the shopkeeper noticed. "Mesmerized."

The fat shopkeeper grinned. "This is terrific. I haven't sold any of my life jackets in a year." He said loudly, "I order both of you to buy a life jacket."

Dr. Drabble brought out his wallet and paid for two life jackets.

The fat shopkeeper grinned again. "I order you to buy these rubber boots and fishing poles. You never know when it will flood in the desert."

Dr. Drabble paid more money.

"Ha! Ha!" the shopkeeper gloated. "This proves you *can* sell life jackets in the desert."

He hummed a happy song and snapped his fingers to the beat. The snapping broke the trance.

"Why are you wearing a life jacket?" Arnie asked.

Dr. Drabble frowned. "The last thing I remember is PJ pointing my Astounding Musical Mesmerizer at us."

Arnie was puzzled. "Why would PJ be mean enough to mesmerize us?"

Two policemen suddenly appeared. "Aha!" the first one said. "We have been searching the entire city for you."

"Yes," the second one said. "By acting crazy, you have scared many people. Imagine grown men singing 'Rock-a-Bye Baby' to each other."

Dr. Drabble turned very red. "We did that?" he whispered to Arnie.

The first policeman said, "See. You are also wearing life jackets here in the desert. That definitely proves you are crazy. We must lock you up to protect the people of this city."

Just then PJ and Chelsea arrived.

"Look what you've done," Arnie said crossly. "You got us arrested."

PJ thought quickly, then brought the Astounding Musical Mesmerizer to his mouth. He could mesmerize the policemen into leaving!

"No," Dr. Drabble commanded. "It is wrong to use that on people for your own convenience."

"I'm sorry," PJ said as the police led the grown-ups away. "I was mad at you for scaring me. It made me feel stupid. So I mesmerized you."

Dr. Drabble looked at PJ gently. "I'm sorry I scared you. I'm just glad you have discovered that revenge is wrong."

Arnie gave PJ a dirty handkerchief to wipe his tears. Then he told the children how Jesus had always forgiven His enemies and wanted us to as well.

"But Dr. Drabble is not even my enemy, and I did something so terrible!" PJ started crying harder.

Suddenly the policemen stopped. "They were mesmerized?"

"Yes," Chelsea said for PJ.

The policemen looked at each other, then they burst into laughter. "Oh, go!" they said. "You are not crazy after all. But please don't do it again."

You can be sure PJ never did.